The Store-Bought Doll

By Lois Meyer • Illustrated by Ruth Sanderson

A GOLDEN BOOK • NEW YORK
Western Publishing Company, Inc., Racine, Wisconsin 53404

Adapted from a story by Clara Louise Grant

Once there was a girl named Christina who lived on a farm with her mother and father.

Christina had a red-and-white rubber ball. She had a skipping rope and a calico beanbag.

Best of all, she had a rag doll named Lucy that her mother had made for her.

Every morning Christina helped milk
the cow and feed the chickens.

Then she helped dry the dishes and sweep the kitchen.

And every afternoon
Christina played with Lucy.
She gave Lucy rides
in the old wheelbarrow.

She had tea parties with Lucy. They used walnut
shells for cups and little flat rocks for pretend
cookies.

She climbed the apple tree
with Lucy and told her special
secrets.

And every night, after she ate supper and had a bath, Christina took Lucy to bed with her. She hugged Lucy and held her tight until they both fell asleep.

One day a man came to Christina's house. He was wearing a fine suit and a silk tie.

"I'm having trouble with my automobile," he told Christina's father. "May I borrow some tools?"

"Of course," said Christina's father. "Maybe I can help you, too." He got his toolbox from the shed, and he and the man went down the road to fix the car.

A little while later, Christina's father and the man
drove up in a shiny automobile.

"Thank you again," said the man as Christina's
father got out of the car.

"Glad I could help," said Christina's father.

The next day the man in the automobile came back.

"You were so kind to help me yesterday," he said. "I wanted to give you something in return. So I've brought a present for your little girl."

It was a china doll. It had blue eyes that opened and closed, and silky yellow hair, and rosy cheeks and lips. It had on a pink satin dress with pearl buttons, and real leather slippers.

Christina could hardly believe her eyes. "It's so beautiful," she said. "I never had a real store-bought doll before. Oh, thank you!"

While the grownups sat on the porch and drank lemonade, Christina ran off to play with her new doll. She left Lucy lying in a heap on the steps.

Christina brushed the doll's
silky yellow hair.

She unbuttoned all the
pearl buttons on the pink
dress. Then she buttoned
them up again.

She rocked the doll in her arms and watched its
eyes close and open.

But she couldn't give the china doll a ride in the wheelbarrow, because she was afraid the pink satin dress would get dirty.

She couldn't have a tea party with the china doll, because she was afraid the walnut shells and rock cookies would scratch its rosy cheeks and lips.

And she couldn't climb the apple tree with the
china doll, because she was afraid the doll would
fall and break.

Late in the afternoon, Christina stood on the
porch with her mother and father and waved
good-by to the kind man as he drove away.

And that night, after she ate supper and had a bath, Christina put the beautiful new doll in a corner of her room. Then she crept downstairs and picked up dear old Lucy. She took Lucy up to bed and held her tighter than ever until they both fell asleep.